STORY COLLECTION

Bath · New York · Singapore · Hong Kong · Cologne · Delhi · Melbourne

TABLE OF CONTENTS

THE LITTLE MERMAID
Ariel's True Love 9

SNOW WHITE AND THE SEVEN DWARFS
Friends to Count On 25

BEAUTY AND THE BEAST
An Enchanted Place 43

CINDERELLA
The Mice Save the Day 59

MULAN
A Time for Courage 77

ALADDIN
The Princess Who Didn't Want to Marry 95

SLEEPING BEAUTY
Falling in Love 113

POCAHONTAS
Listen to Your Heart 131

SNOW WHITE AND THE SEVEN DWARFS
A Royal Visit 147

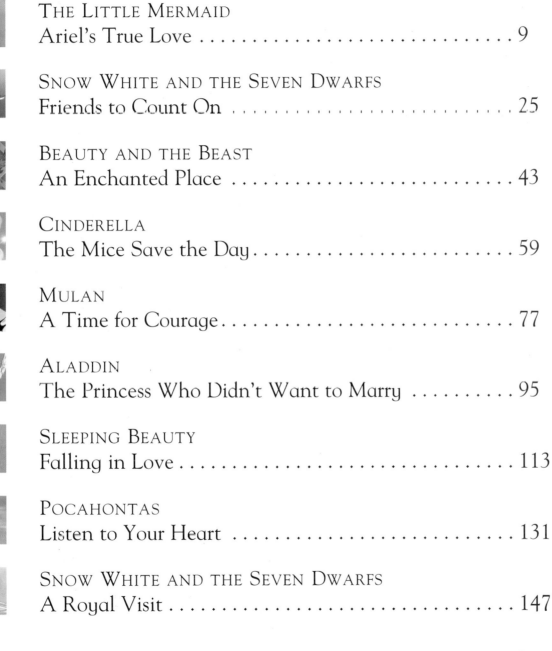

First published by Parragon in 2007
Parragon
Queen Street House
4 Queen Street
Bath BA1 1HE, UK

ISBN 978-1-4054-9835-7

Printed in China

DISNEY's THE LITTLE MERMAID

Ariel's True Love

From deep underwater, a mermaid named Ariel noticed a ship sailing by above. Her father, King Triton, had warned her many times not to go to the ocean's surface. He thought humans were dangerous. But Ariel was fascinated by them: she even had a secret grotto where she kept a collection of human-made treasures, such as candlesticks and pitchers.

Sebastian, a crab who was the king's adviser, noticed the mermaid swimming to the surface. He called to her, but she ignored him. She wanted to know what was happening on the ship.

At the surface, she saw a man being presented with a statue. The other sailors called him Prince Eric.

Ariel sighed. The prince was incredibly handsome. And the statue looked just like him.

Suddenly, the clouds in front of the moon thickened. A strong wind blew across the ocean and lightning crackled in the sky.

"Hurricane a-comin'!" a sailor shouted.

Waves washed over the deck and the ship was tossed on the sea. Lightning struck the main mast and sent it crashing to the deck in flames. Soon the whole ship was on fire. Then it exploded and Prince Eric was thrown overboard!

Ariel swam towards the wreck. She had to find the prince and save him! She spotted him floating on a plank of wood. Prince Eric slipped off of the board and sank beneath the waves. Ariel dived after him and used all of her strength to pull him to the surface.

11

Before long, the sky cleared and Ariel dragged the prince onto the beach. She watched over him, concerned.

"He's so beautiful," she whispered. Then she began to sing to him. Eric's eyes opened and he caught sight of Ariel. But a second later, she was gone. She had returned to the ocean so he wouldn't find out that she was a mermaid.

Later, the prince made his way back to the palace. "A girl rescued me," he told his friend Grimsby. "She was singing. She had the most beautiful voice."

Meanwhile, beneath the waves, Ariel was thinking about Eric, too. She daydreamed and planned ways to see him again. The little mermaid was in love.

Flounder, a blue-and-yellow fish who was Ariel's best friend, led her to the grotto to show her a surprise – it was the statue of Eric!

"Oh, Flounder," Ariel cried. "You're the best!"

Ariel only had a few moments to admire the statue before her father stormed in. He had found out that Ariel had been to the surface and he was furious!

"Contact between the human world and the merworld is strictly forbidden," he scolded her. King Triton lifted his trident and took aim at the human objects.

"Daddy, no!" Ariel cried.

A golden ray shot out from the trident and destroyed a globe. Another blast shattered a candelabrum, then a painting and some books. Finally, Triton turned his trident on the statue, which exploded into pieces.

Ariel burst into tears. Her father didn't seem to understand how important these things were to her. "Just go away!" she said.

Ariel was hurt that her father had destroyed her treasures. She knew he would never allow her to see Eric. So she decided to go and see Ursula, the sea witch.

Ursula made a bargain with the mermaid. She would give Ariel legs for three days. During that time, Ariel had to get Eric to fall in love with her. If he kissed her, she would remain human, but if not, she would turn back into a mermaid – and belong to Ursula for the rest of her life.

"You can't get something for nothing," the sea witch told her. "What I want from you is your voice!"

Ursula took Ariel's voice and put it in her shell necklace. The mermaid would have to get Eric to kiss her without even speaking to him!

Now human, Ariel swam to the beach. Her friend Scuttle the

16

seagull found a ship's sail and some rope and made her a dress. Soon, Eric discovered her.

"You seem very familiar to me," he said. "Have we met?" For a moment, Eric thought she had rescued him from the shipwreck, but then he realized that she was unable to speak. "Then you couldn't be who I thought," he said, disappointed.

Prince Eric took Ariel back to his castle anyway. She tried to adjust to life on land, but everything was so strange! She combed her hair with a fork and accidentally blew soot all over Grimsby with a pipe. Eric couldn't help but laugh.

Grimsby was glad to see the prince enjoying himself. "You know, Eric, perhaps our young guest might enjoy seeing some of the sights of the kingdom," he suggested.

"It's not a bad idea." The prince turned to Ariel. "Well, what do you say? Would you like to join me on a tour of my kingdom tomorrow?"

She nodded happily. It was like a dream come true.

The next morning, the two of them set off in the royal carriage. Ariel was thrilled. The world around her was so exciting and new! She and Eric stopped for a puppet show in town. Ariel got a new hat, two loaves of bread, boots and some flowers. A few hours later, they climbed back into the carriage. After Eric had been driving for a while, Ariel took the reins. She snapped them sharply and the horse took off!

Ariel loved being human and Eric was enchanted by her.

That evening, from a rowing boat in a quiet lagoon, Ariel and Eric watched the sun set.

"I feel bad not knowing your name," Eric said. "Maybe I could guess." He started listing names. "Is it Mildred? Diana? Rachel?" Ariel shook her head. Then Sebastian, who was keeping a close eye on the king's daughter, went to the side of the rowing boat and whispered her name into Eric's ear.

"Ariel?" the prince asked.

She nodded and took his hand. Eric leaned in. Ariel closed her eyes and . . .

Splash!

Eric and Ariel toppled into the water. Ursula had sent her pet

eels to overturn the boat. The

sea witch would do

whatever she could to

keep the two from

kissing!

"Whoa! Hang on.

I've got you." Eric pulled

Ariel back into the boat. But the

romantic moment had passed.

That night, Eric heard the voice of the girl who'd rescued him.

He went to find her and soon he had – she was named Vanessa.

However, the girl was really Ursula in disguise. She was using

Ariel's voice to trick the prince into falling in love with her.

By the next morning, word spread around the kingdom. Eric

was getting married – to Vanessa!

Ariel watched, heartbroken, as the wedding ship set sail. Not only would she never kiss Eric, but tonight he would marry another girl.

Then her friends brought terrible news. They had discovered that Vanessa was really Ursula!

Ariel knew that she had to stop the wedding. She jumped into the water, but without her tail she didn't know how to swim. Flounder pulled her along as she floated on some barrels. "Don't worry, Ariel," he said. "We're going to make it!"

Just as Ariel reached the ship, Scuttle pulled at the shell necklace holding her voice. It fell from Vanessa's neck and broke. Ariel's voice returned to her. "Eric?" she asked.

"Ariel?" Eric said. "It was you all the time!"

He moved towards her to give her a kiss . . . but it was too late! The sun set and Ariel became a mermaid again. Ursula

pulled her into the water.

"I lost her once. I'm not going to lose her again!" Eric cried. He battled the powerful sea witch and destroyed her.

Afterwards, the prince lay on the shore, exhausted. Ariel watched him from afar. King Triton surfaced and looked at his daughter. He realized how much she loved Prince Eric. Happily, he granted Ariel her greatest wish – he gave her legs, so she could be human.

Ariel was thrilled. She and Eric were married immediately. At last they kissed, it was a kiss of true love, joining them together, forever and ever.

Walt Disney's
Snow White
and the Seven Dwarfs
Friends to Count On

Once upon a time, there lived a lovely princess named Snow White. Her wicked stepmother, the Queen, dreaded that someday Snow White would be more beautiful than she was.

Every day, the Queen asked her magic mirror, "Who is the fairest one of all?" And every day the mirror replied, "You are."

One day, the mirror gave a different answer. "Snow White," it said.

The Queen was enraged. She ordered the royal huntsman to take Snow White into the woods and kill her.

That way, the Queen would be the most beautiful woman in the kingdom again. But the Huntsman couldn't bring himself to harm Snow White. When they got to the forest, he told the princess how much the Queen hated her. "Run away," he told her. "Hide."

Snow White turned and ran away as quickly as she could.

The wood was a scary place. Branches seemed to reach for her and roots tripped her. She felt as if eyes were staring at her from the darkness. Snow White screamed. Then she fell and buried her head in fear.

27

In the morning, Snow White lifted her head. She saw eyes watching her, but this time they were the friendly eyes of bunnies, deer, chipmunks, birds and raccoons. Snow White was glad she wasn't alone any more. "Please don't run away," she said. "I won't hurt you."

Snow White knew she could never return to the castle. What would she do? Where would she go? Maybe the animals can help me, she thought.

"I need a place to sleep at night," she said. The animals looked at each other. The birds took her cape in their beaks and guided her forwards. Soon they came to a clearing in the woods. Beneath the trees stood a charming little cottage.

"Just like a dollhouse!" Snow White cried. She peeked in the window. No one was home. The animals nodded at her, seeming to say it was all right for her to go inside.

Snow White pushed the door open. Inside the cottage, dishes were piled high in the sink and clothes were tossed about. The floor hadn't been swept in ages. Snow White counted the tiny chairs at the table and decided seven children must live in the cottage. "Seven untidy children," she said with a shake of her head.

Snow White grabbed a broom. "We'll clean the house and surprise them," she said to the animals. "Then maybe they'll let me stay."

She started to sweep, singing the whole time. The raccoons washed clothes, the deer dusted and the chipmunks tidied. In no time, the room was spotless.

After the cleaning had been done, Snow White became curious about the rest of the cottage. "Let's see what's up the stairs," she said. She lit a candle and climbed up the steps. At the top was a door. Snow White opened it and went into a room with seven little beds. Each bed had a name carved on it.

"Doc, Happy, Sneezy, Dopey," Snow White said with a laugh. "What funny names for children!" She read on. "Grumpy, Bashful and Sleepy."

By then, Snow White was feeling awfully sleepy herself. She lay down across three of the small beds. The birds covered her with a blanket and minutes later the princess was fast asleep.

31

Before long, the owners of the cottage returned. They were not children at all – they were Dwarfs.

When they opened the door, they couldn't believe their eyes! "The whole house is clean!" Doc exclaimed. Nervously, the Dwarfs tiptoed upstairs. They thought an intruder was in their room!

They went in and Doc slowly pulled away the blanket that had been covering Snow White.

"Why, it's a girl!" he cried.

"An angel," whispered Bashful.

But Grumpy thought differently. "All females are poison!" he insisted.

As Snow White began to wake up, the nervous Dwarfs hid behind the beds. They peeked at her over the footboards.

The princess yawned and sat up. Startled, she caught sight of the Dwarfs' faces. "Oh, you're little men!" she cried. "Now don't tell me who you are. Let me guess." One by one, she matched the names on the beds to the Dwarfs. She got all of them right the first time.

Snow White told the Dwarfs how she had run through the woods and that the Queen wanted to kill her.

"Send her away!" Grumpy warned the other Dwarfs. He was worried that the Queen might use an evil magic spell on them.

"She won't find me here," the princess promised. "I'll wash and keep house and cook. . . ."

The Dwarfs imagined the apple dumplings and gooseberry pies that Snow White could make. "She stays!" they agreed. Then they followed her downstairs.

That night, after a delicious dinner, the Dwarfs and Snow White yodelled and sang. Dopey played the drums, Sleepy played the horn and Grumpy played the pipe organ. Snow White clapped along to the music. Then she danced with her new friends. The Dwarfs had never had so much fun or laughed so hard!

When they stopped singing and dancing, Sleepy turned to Snow White. "Tell us a story," he said.

Snow White told them about a princess who had fallen in love with a prince she'd met at a wishing well. "Was it you?" they asked and she nodded. Her dearest wish was to see him again some day.

Sighing dreamily, the Dwarfs let Snow White sleep in their cosy beds for the night. Bashful slept in a drawer and Happy climbed into a cupboard. Doc chose the sink, while Grumpy hopped in a large pot. The Dwarfs didn't mind – even Grumpy was glad that Snow White had stayed.

In the morning, the Dwarfs got ready to go to work in the mines. They were worried about leaving Snow White alone, especially after what the Queen had tried to do to her.

"I'll be all right," Snow White said. Then she kissed each of the Dwarfs good-bye.

"I'm warnin' ya . . . don't let nobody or nothin' in the house!" Grumpy ordered.

"Oh, Grumpy, you do care!" Snow White exclaimed and gave him a big kiss. He stomped away, pretending to be mad, but he had a goofy smile on his face.

That afternoon, forgetting Grumpy's warning, Snow White allowed a poor old woman into the house.

The woman gave her an apple, perfectly red and shiny. "Go on, have a bite," she urged. But the apple was not an ordinary apple and the old woman was not an ordinary woman. She was the evil Queen in disguise and the fruit had been poisoned!

Snow White's animal friends tried to warn her not to trust the woman, but she didn't understand. She reached out, raised the apple to her lips and took a bite.

"Oh, I feel strange," she cried and fell to the floor.

When the Dwarfs returned to the house, they found their friend and thought she was dead. They had no way of knowing that the spell the Queen had used was for a sleeping death, or that Love's First Kiss could wake Snow White up.

The Dwarfs could not bear to lose the princess. They built her a beautiful coffin of gold and glass and set it in the woods where all of her animal friends could visit her.

One day, a prince came by – the same prince that Snow White had met by the Wishing Well! He gazed at the girl in the glass coffin and knew her as the princess he loved. The Prince lifted the glass lid, bent down and kissed her.

Slowly, she awakened. The Prince lifted her in his arms. Around them, the Dwarfs and animals danced and hugged and jumped for joy. Their friend was alive again – and her true love had found her!

"Good-bye," Snow White said and kissed each of the Dwarfs. She was leaving to marry the Prince, but she knew she would visit her good friends again soon.

An Enchanted Place

Once upon a time, there lived a beautiful young girl named Belle. She loved to read and could often be seen wandering through her village with a book in her hand.

Belle lived with her father, Maurice, who was an inventor. One day, he went to a fair. On the way home, a bad storm broke out and he took shelter inside a dark castle. But the master of the castle was an angry beast and once he discovered Maurice, he

would not let him leave!

Belle searched for her father when he didn't return home. She soon came to the castle and went inside. "Hello? Is anyone here?" she called as she walked through the hallways.

A wooden mantel clock and a fancy candelabrum were sitting on one of the tables. Belle didn't notice them, but they noticed her.

"It's a girl!" cried Lumiere the candelabrum, once Belle had

passed. He jumped to the floor. "She's the one! The girl we have been waiting for! She's come to break the spell!"

Many years earlier, Lumiere and Cogsworth, the clock, had been human, along with lots of the other objects in the castle. But their master, the prince and his

castle had been put under a spell. The servants had been changed into enchanted objects, such as the clock and the candelabrum, while the prince had been turned into an awful beast. The spell could only be broken if, by his twenty-first year, the Beast fell in love with a girl who loved him back.

Lumiere and Cogsworth followed Belle. Before long, she came to the dungeon where her father was locked up.

"Papa!" she exclaimed. She knelt down to touch his hand.

"You must go!" Maurice cried. But already it was too late – the Beast had entered the room.

Belle was not afraid, though. "I've come for my father. Please let him out," she said sternly.

"He's my prisoner," the Beast growled.

"Take me instead," Belle offered.

"You would take his place?" the Beast asked, astonished.

Belle agreed and the Beast dragged Maurice from his cell and sent him away.

On his way back to the dungeon, Lumiere suggested that his master find Belle a more comfortable place to stay than the cold, dark cell.

The Beast was not hard-hearted, though his manners were rough and his temper terrible. When he saw Belle sobbing, he softened. "Follow me," he demanded and led her to a much nicer room.

"Dinner!" Lumiere whispered in the Beast's ear. "Invite her to dinner!"

"You will join me for dinner!" the Beast commanded before he slammed the door shut.

Soon, some of the servants stopped by to introduce themselves. Mrs Potts, the teapot and her son, Chip – a teacup, offered Belle a spot of tea. She was surprised that the servants were

enchanted objects, but she liked them at once. They couldn't convince her to go to dinner, though.

Cogsworth finally broke the bad news to the Beast. "She's not coming," he said.

The Beast went to Belle's room and pounded on the door. "I thought I told you to come down to dinner!" he growled.

"I'm not hungry," Belle replied.

"Please," Cogsworth quietly urged the Beast, "attempt to be a gentleman."

"It would give me great pleasure if you would join me for dinner," the Beast managed.

But Belle still said no. She would not eat with the creature who was holding her captive. The Beast stormed off. "If she doesn't eat with me, then she doesn't eat at all!" he roared.

Later that night, Belle sneaked out of her room and tiptoed downstairs.

When she went to the kitchen, a strange sight met her eyes. All the dishes, pots and pans, the stove and the silverware were alive, just like the other objects she'd met.

They had been upset when she'd refused to come to dinner because they were eager to impress her. There were never guests at the castle any more.

"I am a little hungry," Belle admitted.

"You are?" asked Mrs Potts, who had been the castle cook. "Wake the china! I'm not about to let the poor child go hungry."

Belle had been hoping for a bite to eat. Instead, she got a full-blown feast. Beef and cheese, pie and pudding – Belle had never had such a meal! Her new friends treated her like a princess.

After dinner, Belle wanted to explore. "It's my first time in an enchanted castle," she told the servants.

Cogsworth and Lumiere led her around, showing her paintings, tapestries and armour.

"What's up there?" Belle asked when they came to a very long staircase.

It was the west wing and everyone was forbidden to go there. Cogsworth and Lumiere tried to lead Belle in another direction, but she slipped by them and climbed the steps. Behind the door at the top was a wreck of a room. Furniture was torn apart. A painting of a handsome prince was ripped down the middle.

The only thing intact was a single rose under glass and even its petals had started to fall off. Once the last petal fell from the rose, the spell over the castle could never be broken! But Belle didn't know about the spell.

Suddenly, the Beast's shadow fell over her.

"Get out!" he yelled and started to smash things.

Belle ran down the stairs and past Lumiere and Cogsworth. "Promise or no promise," she cried, "I can't stay here another minute!" She dashed out of the front door, grabbed her horse and rode into the dark forest. But the forest was not safe, it was full of wolves that chased after Belle. She tried to hold them back with a stick, but they snapped it in two.

Suddenly, the Beast appeared. He growled at the wolves and tossed them left and right. They bit his neck and clawed at his fur, but he managed to fight them off. At last, the wolves ran away.

Since the Beast had been hurt while protecting her, Belle didn't feel right about leaving. She took him back to the castle and nursed his wounds. "Thank you for saving my life," she said.

Day by day, the Beast and Belle got to know each other better. They ate together. They played in the snow together. One day, the Beast shared his library with her. She had never seen so many books! And one evening, they danced together!

The servants were overjoyed. They could tell the Beast was falling in love with Belle . . . and Belle with the Beast.

But Belle was very concerned about her father's health. She wanted to see him.

Because the Beast loved her, he decided to let her go, even though it meant he wouldn't be able to break the spell.

With a last glance towards the Beast, Belle left the castle and went to her father.

The villagers heard that the Beast had captured Belle, they attacked the castle, even though she'd told them how nice he'd been.

Lumiere and Cogsworth came up with a plan to defend the castle. When the villagers stormed inside, some of the enchanted furniture fell on them. Teacups poured scalding tea on their heads, cabinet doors flew open and knocked people down and knives and forks soared through the air. The villagers ran out of the gates, screaming.

During the fighting, the Beast was badly hurt. Belle returned to the castle to find him wounded and dying.

"Beast!" she cried, kneeling beside him.

"Belle," he said, gasping. "You came back!" He was weak though, and soon his eyes closed.

"Please don't leave me!" Belle sobbed. Then, just in time, she added three magic words: "I love you."

Tiny comets showered down on the Beast. As Belle watched, the Beast's claws became hands and his fur changed to human skin. He became the prince he once had been and would be again, now that Belle had broken the spell.

"Belle, it's me," he said.

She looked deep into his eyes. "It is you!" she cried happily.

Cogsworth, Lumiere, Mrs Potts, Chip and all of the other servants returned to their human forms too.

Belle leaned in and kissed her prince.

"Are they gonna live happily ever after, Mama?" Chip asked.

"Of course, dear," Mrs Potts said with a happy sigh. "Of course."

Walt Disney's
Cinderella

The Mice Save the Day

One day, Gus, Jaq and the other mice who lived in Lady Tremaine's château gathered around their friend Cinderella as she pulled her mother's old dress out of a trunk.

"Isn't it lovely?" Cinderella said. "Well, maybe it is a little old-fashioned," she added, "but I can fix that!"

Earlier that day, the mice had watched as an invitation to a royal ball had arrived. Since Cinderella's father had died, her stepmother, Lady Tremaine, forced her to do all of the housework. But her stepmother had promised that Cinderella could go to the ball if she finished her chores and found something presentable to wear. Her mother's old dress needed a few alterations, which wouldn't be difficult – if Cinderella could find the time to do them.

"Cinderellllaa!" her stepmother and stepsisters called. They were getting ready for the ball and wouldn't give Cinderella a moment's peace. Plus, she still had to do all of her chores.

"I guess my dress will just have to wait," she sighed sadly.

After she left the attic, Jaq said, "Know what? Cinderelly not go to the ball."

The other mice looked at him, startled. Cinderella's bird friends, who were perched on the attic windowsill, twittered anxiously.

"Work, work, work!" he explained with disgust. "She'll never get her dress done."

Cinderella's animal friends decided to surprise her by fixing the dress. After all, she had been caring for them for years. Just that day, she had rescued poor Gus from a mousetrap. Then she had given him a new shirt and fed him. Every day she made sure her mouse and bird friends got enough to eat.

The mice and birds worked together to make Cinderella's dress the most beautiful at the ball. First, they measured the gown's skirt. Jaq and Gus used scissors to cut a long swatch of pink fabric. Flying through the air, the birds draped the fabric across the back of the dress. More birds hoisted the mice into the air so that they could sew the fabric into place.

Then the mice hefted sewing needles over their shoulders and stitched on pretty ruffles. The birds draped on shiny ribbons. As a finishing touch, Gus and Jaq found a sash and a string of beads that the stepsisters had thrown away.

The birds and mice completed the dress just as the carriages arrived to take Lady Tremaine and her two daughters to the ball.

Cinderella sadly climbed the stairs to her attic room, sure she wouldn't be able to attend. But when she opened the door, her animal friends called out, "Surprise!"

"Oh, thank you so much!" Cinderella exclaimed. The birds and mice were overjoyed to see their friend so happy. She was always working so hard.

When Cinderella ran downstairs in her new dress, her stepsisters and stepmother were very surprised. They hadn't thought Cinderella would find anything to wear.

"We did make a bargain, didn't we, Cinderella?" her stepmother said.

Suddenly suspicious, Jaq and Gus watched from a mouse hole in the wall.

"Those beads give it just the right touch, don't you think, Drizella?" Cinderella's stepmother asked.

"Why, you little thief!" cried Drizella. She lunged and ripped the beads off of Cinderella's neck.

"Look, that's my sash!" Anastasia piped up.

The girls tore Cinderella's lovely dress to shreds and then flounced out of the door to their carriage. Cinderella ran to the garden crying, her hopes dashed.

Cinderella's animal friends gathered around her as she wept on a stone bench. They wished they could comfort her.

Suddenly, Cinderella heard an unfamiliar voice say: "There, there. Dry your tears."

It was Cinderella's Fairy Godmother! Waving her magic wand, the Fairy Godmother turned a pumpkin into a magnificent coach.

Cinderella stared in amazement as the Fairy Godmother continued to work her magic. "Bibbidi-Bobbidi-Boo!" she cried. Soon, four of the mice, including Gus and Jaq, had turned into white horses. Bruno the dog became the footman and the stable horse became the coachman.

Then the Fairy Godmother looked at Cinderella's torn dress. "Good heavens, child!" she exclaimed. "You can't go to the ball in that!" She waved her wand once more. Suddenly, Cinderella was wearing beautiful glass slippers and a blue ball gown that shimmered like diamonds. Even her hair was arranged elegantly. She gazed at her reflection in the fountain with disbelief.

"It's more than I ever hoped for!" she declared, her eyes sparkling.

The Fairy Godmother helped Cinderella climb into the coach. "You must understand, my dear, on the stroke of twelve the spell will be broken."

When she arrived at the palace, Cinderella felt as though she were in a dream world. Everyone wondered who this mysterious girl was.

The handsome young prince bowed before her and Cinderella felt her heart pounding. Later, he swept her into his arms and they danced together in the castle garden.

Gazing into her eyes, the Prince leaned down to kiss her just as the clock struck twelve. When she heard the bell toll, Cinderella remembered the Fairy Godmother's warning. She raced down the grand staircase, accidentally leaving one of her dainty glass slippers behind.

The next day, Cinderella went about her chores. She daydreamed and hummed a waltz as she worked. Cinderella's mouse friends tried to warn her to be careful, but she was too busy thinking of the Prince.

Lady Tremaine overheard Cinderella and recognized the song from the ball. She realized that Cinderella was the girl from the ball who'd danced with the Prince all evening. Her stepmother locked her in her attic room.

"No! Please let me out!" cried Cinderella.

"We've got to get that key," Jaq told Gus. The two mice raced downstairs and quietly took the key out of the stepmother's pocket. Then they pushed and pulled it up the long staircase. With a last burst of energy, Cinderella's exhausted little friends were finally able to slip the key under her locked door.

"Oh, thank you!" she cried.

Cinderella hurried down the steps. The Grand Duke had arrived while she was locked in the attic. He was searching for the Prince's mysterious love by trying the glass slipper on every maiden in the kingdom, including Cinderella's stepsisters.

"Wait, please wait!" she called to the Grand Duke.

At the sound of Cinderella's voice, everyone looked up. The mice hugged each other hopefully. But Cinderella's stepmother was upset that her stepchild had escaped and she tripped the Grand Duke with her walking stick. The slipper Cinderella had left behind at the ball shattered!

Luckily, Cinderella still had the other slipper. She pulled it out of her pocket, then tried it on.

74

The slipper's perfect fit proved that
Cinderella was the beautiful young
woman who had won the Prince's
heart. The Prince asked for
Cinderella's hand in
marriage and the very
next day they had
their wedding at
the palace.

Gus, Jaq and the other mice were thrilled that Cinderella had found her true love. Cinderella insisted that her loyal animal friends move to the palace with her. They gladly left Lady Tremaine's château behind and began a new life as royal mice.

A Time for Courage

Long ago and far beyond the Great Wall of China, a young woman named Fa Mulan lived with her family.

One day, the Emperor's aide rode into town. "The Huns have invaded China!" he announced. "One man from every family must serve in the Imperial Army."

Mulan's father felt it was his duty to join the army even though he had been injured in earlier battles. That night, he began to practise some fighting moves, unaware that Mulan was watching. Suddenly, a pain from an old wound shot through his leg and he collapsed on the floor.

Mulan knew that her father wouldn't be able to survive another battle, so she decided to disguise herself as a man and take his place. She cut her hair, put on soldier's clothing and left in the middle of the night on her horse, Khan.

But Mulan was not alone. The spirits of her ancestors sent Mushu, a tiny dragon, along to protect her.

Mushu caught up with Mulan and soon they arrived at the army camp. Mushu whispered suggestions about how to look more like a man. "Show them your man walk," he said. "Shoulders back, chest high, feet apart, head up and strut."

"I don't think I can do this," whispered Mulan.

"It's all attitude," Mushu told her.

Mulan took a deep breath, gathered her courage and strode into camp.

She looked ridiculous, but she did her best. When she tried to make friends with the other soldiers, Chien-Po, Yao and Ling, she ended up causing a fight.

The camp was in total chaos when Captain Shang arrived.

"Soldiers!" the captain shouted.

Everyone sprang to attention and pointed at Mulan. "He started it!" they said in unison.

"I don't need anyone causing trouble in my camp," Shang said to Mulan.

"Sorry," Mulan said. Then she remembered she was supposed to be a man and lowered her voice. "I, uh, mean, sorry."

"What's your name?" Shang asked.

"My name is . . . uh . . . Ping," Mulan told him. She handed him her army papers and frowned. She was not off to a good start.

Captain Shang was a skilful leader and though Mulan felt clumsy and inadequate, she worked as hard as she could. She didn't want anyone to find out that she was a girl.

Shang led the recruits through a series of gruelling training exercises to help them prepare for battle. One of the lessons involved retrieving an arrow from the top of a pole with a heavy bronze disc tied to each wrist.

"One represents discipline, the other strength," Shang said of the discs. "You need both to reach the arrow."

No one was able to do it. Finally, after several attempts, Mulan had an idea. She pulled the weights onto her wrists, looped them together and used them to hoist herself to the top. She had done it!

All of the soldiers admired Mulan's determination. And even her new friends, Chien-Po, Ling and Yao, still didn't know that she wasn't a man.

After much training, Shang led the soldiers to the Tung-Shao Pass to meet the rest of the army. When they arrived, they discovered that the army had been defeated – and none of the soldiers had survived. Shang was especially upset when he realized that his father, the General, had been killed.

"I'm sorry," Mulan said, trying to comfort him.

Shang composed himself and turned to his soldiers. "The Huns are moving quickly. We're the only hope for the Emperor now. Move out!" he ordered.

Before long, the Huns discovered Shang and his troops. Hundreds of them raced over the mountaintop, firing arrows at Shang's small band of soldiers. Mulan seized a cannon and ran right towards the Huns. When she had almost reached their leader, Shan-Yu, Mulan aimed the cannon above his head. The rocket hit the mountain behind him and caused a huge avalanche. Snow tumbled down quickly, burying the enemy.

Mulan had been wounded, but she was still able to jump on her horse and pull Shang away from the snow just before he was buried.

As Chien-Po and the others helped them to safety, Shang looked at Mulan with admiration. "Ping, you are the craziest man I've ever met. For that, I owe you my life," he said. "From now on you have my trust."

But Mulan's wound had to be treated. It was then that the soldiers learned that she was really a woman.

At that time in China, Mulan's deception was punishable by death. Shang spared her. "A life for a life," he declared. "My debt is repaid." He told her she would not be allowed to continue on with the other soldiers.

Dejected, Mulan watched the troops march away, leaving her alone with Mushu and Khan. With a heavy heart, she confided in the dragon: "I should never have left home. I just wanted to do things right, so that when I looked in the mirror I would see someone worthwhile. But I was wrong. I see nothing."

"You risked your life to help the people you love," Mushu replied. "But don't worry, things will work out."

That quiet moment was shattered when Mulan realized that Shan-Yu and a few of the Huns had survived. Racing on horseback to the Imperial City, Mulan found Shang and told him what she had seen.

"You don't belong here," he replied. "Go home."

"You have to believe me," said Mulan.

But Shang wouldn't listen. Soon, the Huns seized the Emperor and ran into the palace. Mulan turned to her friends for help. Chien-Po, Ling and Yao tried to break down the palace door. It was no use.

"Hey, I have an idea!" Mulan called. Eager for the help of their quick-thinking friend, the soldiers let Mulan dress them up as women. Then they used the sashes from their dresses to help them climb the palace columns. Shang realized that Mulan was trustworthy and joined their effort. Once inside, they attacked the unsuspecting Huns.

Together, Mulan, Shang and the others knocked out the Hun soldiers and rescued the Emperor. Then Shang went after Shan-Yu. Furious that the Emperor had escaped, the Hun leader drew his sword.

"You took away my victory," Shan-Yu growled at Shang.

"No," said Mulan. "I did." She pulled back her hair so that Shan-Yu would recognize her and Shang's life would be spared.

"The soldier from the mountains!" the Hun leader cried. He began to chase her.

Leading Shan-Yu to the top of the palace, Mulan grabbed his sword and pinned his cloak to the roof. Mushu shot towards him on a rocket. The little dragon jumped to safety just before the rocket blasted Shan-Yu into a tower of fireworks.

After the battle, the Emperor approached Mulan. "I have heard a great deal about you, Fa Mulan," he said. "You stole your father's armour, ran away from home, impersonated a soldier, deceived your commanding officer, dishonoured the Chinese army, destroyed my palace, and . . . you have saved us all."

Then, he bowed to Mulan in gratitude. Stunned, everyone else did the same. "See to it that this woman is made a member of my council," the Emperor told his aide.

Mulan was honoured but knew that she needed to return to her family.

"Then take this, so your family will know what you have done for me," the Emperor said, handing her a pendant with his crest on it. Then he gave her Shan-Yu's sword. "And this, so the world will know what you have done for China."

Mulan thanked the Emperor and said good-bye to her friends. It was time to go home and face her father.

At home, Mulan presented the Emperor's pendant and Shan-Yu's sword to her father. "They are gifts to honour the Fa family," she explained and bowed her head.

He put them aside and hugged Mulan. "The greatest gift and honour is having you for a daughter," he said.

Shang had followed Mulan home. He realized that his feelings for her had grown. She had been very courageous and he admired her for it.

Mulan invited Shang to stay for dinner. He and her family celebrated, delighted everything had turned out so well.

The Princess Who
Didn't Want to Marry

Princess Jasmine giggled at her pet tiger, Rajah, as she sat by the fountain in the palace courtyard. The tiger had not been impressed with the latest prince to ask for Jasmine's hand in marriage, so he'd helped scare him away. They were both glad to be rid of the selfish suitor, one of many unworthy princes who'd visited recently.

Jasmine's father, the Sultan of Agrabah, was not amused. "Dearest, you've got to stop rejecting every suitor who comes to call," he told his daughter. "The law says you must be married to a prince by your next birthday. You've only got three more days!"

Jasmine thought that the law was unfair. "Father, I hate being forced into this," she said. "If I do marry, I want it to be for love."

Lately she'd found herself wishing she wasn't a princess at all. She had never even been allowed to go outside the palace walls. She felt trapped.

That night, the princess decided to run away. She put on a disguise and began to climb over the palace wall. Rajah tugged on her dress – he didn't want her to leave.

Jasmine knew she would miss her friend, but she had to see what else was out there.

"I'm sorry, Rajah, but I can't stay here and have my life lived for me," she explained.

Rajah nodded and slid his head under Jasmine's foot to give her a boost over the wall.

The next morning, Jasmine arrived at the marketplace. She looked around excitedly, for she had never seen anything like it. People were selling everything from pots and necklaces to fish and figs. As she walked, she came upon a little boy who looked like he hadn't eaten in a while.

"Oh, you must be hungry," Jasmine said. The boy looked up at her eagerly. She took an apple from a nearby stand and handed it to the poor child.

"You'd better be able to pay for that," the apple seller said.

"Pay?" Jasmine said with surprise. She'd never needed to pay for anything at the palace.

"No one steals from my cart!" the vendor bellowed and grabbed her angrily. Jasmine was frightened and didn't know what to do.

Luckily, a handsome stranger came to her rescue.

"Oh, thank you, kind sir," the young man said to the apple seller. "I'm so glad you found her. I've been looking all over."

Jasmine looked puzzled. "What are you doing?" she whispered to the young man. She noticed that he had a pet monkey with him.

"Just play along," he replied.

"You know this girl?" the seller asked him.

"Sadly, yes. She is my sister," he replied. "She's a little crazy. She thinks the monkey is the Sultan."

Jasmine knelt down. "Oh, wise Sultan," she said to the monkey, "how may I serve you?"

"Tragic, isn't it?" the young man said as Jasmine pretended to be crazy. "Now come along, sis. Time to go see the doctor."

They started to leave. It looked like they would escape until the monkey bowed good-bye . . . and a bunch of stolen apples tumbled from his vest!

"Come back here, you little thieves!" the fruit seller yelled.
The trio ran as quickly as they could and finally reached the
young man's rooftop home. They were safe . . . for now.

Jasmine looked around. The stranger's home was simple, but at least it was his own. No one told him what to do. Jasmine couldn't imagine having so much freedom.

At the same time, the young man was looking longingly at the palace in the distance. It would be wonderful to live there, he thought, to have enough money so he wouldn't have to worry about his next meal.

"Sometimes I just feel so trapped," they both said.

Surprised, they looked at each other. Jasmine suddenly felt that she had a lot in common with this handsome stranger. But just then, angry palace guards burst in. Jasmine looked around – there was no escape!

"Do you trust me?" asked the young man, holding out his hand to her.

She looked into his brown eyes and said, "Yes."

"Then, jump!" he cried.

Jasmine took his hand and they leaped off of the roof. They landed safely in a pile of grain, then raced through the marketplace . . . right into another set of guards!

The head guard seized the young man. "It's the dungeon for you, boy!" he declared.

"Unhand him!" demanded Jasmine, pulling down her hood and revealing herself as the princess. The guard was shocked to see her outside the palace walls. "Do as I command," she ordered. "Release him."

"I would, Princess, except my orders come from Jafar," the guard replied. "You'll have to take it up with him."

Jasmine crossed her arms and narrowed her eyes. "Believe me, I will," she said.

Back at the palace, the princess confronted Jafar, one of her father's advisors. The evil man told her that the stranger had been sentenced to death and killed.

"I am exceedingly sorry, Princess," Jafar lied.

Jasmine glared at Jafar. "How could you?" she said and ran out. She went to see her tiger friend. "It's all my fault, Rajah," she said, sobbing. "I didn't even know his name."

The next day, on the streets of Agrabah, there was a magnificent parade. Men playing drums marched down the street, followed by women dancing with scarves. All of the townspeople stopped what they were doing to watch.

Inside the palace, the Sultan heard the music. He went to his balcony and was delighted by what he saw below. "Oh, Jafar!" he called. "You must come and see this!"

Reluctantly, Jafar joined the Sultan.

Trumpets blared and banners waved as the parade made its way to the palace. But most impressive was Prince Ali, who sat on top of an enormous elephant, throwing gold coins into the crowd. He looked attractive, regal – and extremely smug.

Princess Jasmine, who was still upset about the death of the young man from the market, watched from her balcony. She shook her head in disgust at this latest suitor. Did he think he could buy her hand in marriage?

Nevertheless, the Sultan welcomed Prince Ali into the palace. "Your Majesty, I have journeyed from afar to seek your daughter's hand," said Prince Ali after flying in on a magic carpet.

"Prince Ali Ababwa," said the Sultan, "I'm delighted to meet you."

But Jafar had his own sneaky plan: he wanted to marry the princess himself so that someday he would rule the kingdom. He whispered to the Sultan, "What makes him think he is worthy of the princess?"

Confidently, Prince Ali replied, "Just let her meet me. I'll win your daughter."

But Jasmine had been listening and was very upset. "How dare you – all of you! Standing around deciding my future," she cried. "I am not a prize to be won!" She turned and stormed off.

But Prince Ali would not give up. That evening, he appeared on Jasmine's balcony and apologized. Rajah growled protectively and was about to chase him away, but Jasmine thought the prince looked familiar. When she stepped closer, he offered to take her on a magic carpet ride.

"We could get out of the palace . . . see the world," Prince Ali offered.

Jasmine hesitated. "Is it safe?" she asked, looking at the carpet.

Prince Ali leaned forwards, offering his hand. "Do you trust me?" he asked. Jasmine thought he might be the young man from the marketplace! Maybe he hadn't been killed, after all! She gave him her hand and climbed aboard the Magic Carpet.

Jasmine and Prince Ali flew over the streets and rooftops of Agrabah. They held hands and Jasmine felt happier than she ever had.

Jasmine got the prince to admit that he was the young man from the marketplace. But he didn't tell her everything because he didn't think she would like him if she knew the truth. His real name was Aladdin. After escaping from the dungeon, he'd found a magic lamp. The Genie inside had given him three wishes. Aladdin, who had fallen in love with Jasmine, had used one of them to become a prince so he could marry her.

"I sometimes dress as a commoner to escape the pressures of palace life," he lied. "But I really am a prince."

"Why didn't you just tell me?" asked Jasmine.

"Well, you know, uh, royalty going out into the city in disguise . . . it sounds a little strange, don't you think?" he said.

Jasmine looked down. "Not that strange," she said quietly.

Soon after they returned from the romantic Magic Carpet ride, Jafar discovered Prince Ali's secret and revealed his true identity. Then Jafar tried to seize power, but Aladdin and Jasmine fought him bravely and won. Together, they had saved the kingdom.

After the battle, Aladdin took Jasmine's hands in his. "I'm sorry I lied to you about being a prince," he said humbly.

Jasmine held his hands. She hadn't fallen in love with him because she thought he was a prince. She loved him for who he was inside. The princess had finally found someone she wanted to marry. Her father gladly changed the law so that she'd be able to.

Aladdin and Jasmine climbed aboard the Magic Carpet and kissed. Beneath them was a whole new world where they would live together, happily ever after.

Walt Disney's
Sleeping Beauty

Falling in Love

Once upon a time, in a faraway land, there lived a king and queen. They longed to have a child and, after years of waiting, their wish was granted. A daughter was born. They named her Aurora after the dawn, because she filled their life with sunshine.

To celebrate her birth, the king and queen declared a holiday. Guests travelled from near and far to visit the tiny princess, including three good fairies named: Flora, Fauna and Merryweather.

Each fairy would bless the princess with a single, magical gift. Flora blessed the child with beauty. Fauna gave the gift of song. But before Merryweather could cast her spell, a gust of wind blew through the great hall.

In a flash of lightning, a tall, dark figure appeared. It was the evil fairy Maleficent, who was furious that she hadn't been invited to the party.

"I too, have a gift to bestow on the child," she said with a wicked grin. "Before the sun sets on her sixteenth birthday, she shall prick her finger on the spindle of a spinning wheel and die!" With that, she disappeared in a burst of foul green smoke.

The king and queen were panic-stricken. Flora tried to calm them. "Don't despair," she said. "Merryweather still has her gift to give."

Although her magic was not strong enough to undo the curse, Merryweather did have the power to help.

And so, with a wave of her magic wand, Merryweather declared, "Not in death, but just in sleep the fateful prophecy you'll keep. From this slumber you shall wake, when True Love's Kiss the spell shall break."

Still, the fairies thought, perhaps there was an even better way to save the princess from the curse. What if they pretended to be peasant

women and raised the princess as their own in a secret, far-off place for sixteen years? If Maleficent could not find Aurora, how could she harm her?

The king and queen sadly agreed to the plan, knowing it was the only way they could protect their daughter from Maleficent. They watched with heavy hearts as the fairies changed themselves into humans and disappeared into the night with the princess.

By morning, the fairies and the princess arrived at an old cottage deep in the woods, which became their home. The fairies stopped using magic and pretended to be Aurora's aunts. They called her Briar Rose, so that no one would learn of her whereabouts. That would keep her safe from Maleficent.

The years passed quickly and before they knew it, Briar Rose's sixteenth birthday had arrived. To celebrate, the fairies planned a surprise – they would make the girl a beautiful dress and a delicious cake! But first they had to get her out of the cottage. So they sent her to pick berries.

Briar Rose enjoyed strolling through the woods. As she walked, she sang to the forest animals who had become her friends, all the time dreaming of a tall, handsome prince.

Little did she know that a real prince just happened to be riding through the forest that very morning.

"Hear that?" the prince said to his horse, Samson. The sound of Briar Rose's sweet voice had drifted over to him. The prince was enchanted – he had to find out where it was coming from!

Eagerly, he urged his horse into a gallop – but as Samson leaped over a log, the prince fell off. He landed in a creek with a most undignified splash.

"No carrots for you!" he scolded as he climbed out of the water. He laid his hat, cape and boots out to dry. At the same time, he couldn't help but wonder about the voice that he'd heard. It was almost too beautiful to be real.

"Maybe it was some mysterious being," he said, "a wood sprite, or a – "

But his thoughts were interrupted by the shocking sight of his wet clothes beginning to fly and hop away. Briar Rose's animal friends were stealing them!

"Why, it's my dream prince!" Briar Rose laughingly declared when the rabbits and birds appeared before her, dressed in the stolen clothes. "You know, I'm really not supposed to speak to strangers, but we have met before." And while the real prince looked on, hidden behind a nearby tree, Briar Rose began to sing and dance with her dressed-up forest friends.

As Briar Rose turned away, the real prince quickly stepped in. When he began to sing with her, she spun around.

"Oh!" she gasped. Her three aunts were always warning her to stay away from strangers . . . and yet there was something so familiar about this young man (whom she never dreamed was an actual prince). She couldn't help but feel that they had met before.

Long into the afternoon, Briar Rose and the prince sang and danced together and before either one could help it, they had fallen in love.

When Briar Rose finally returned to the surprise party that awaited her at the cottage, it was her aunts who were most surprised.

"This is the happiest day of my life," Briar Rose said with a sigh. Then she told them about the young man she'd just met and how she'd invited him to the cottage that very evening.

"This is terrible," moaned Flora. "You must never see that young man again." She explained to Briar Rose that she was already betrothed – and had been since birth – to a young prince named Phillip.

"But how could I marry a prince?" Briar Rose asked. "I'd have to be . . ."

". . . a princess," Merryweather finished.

The fairies then told Briar Rose about her real parents and her real name. Flora, Fauna and Merryweather changed themselves back into fairies, wrapped the princess in a cloak and set off for the palace immediately.

They arrived at the castle just as the sun began to set. The poor princess was so sad about not being able to see the young man from the forest again that the fairies left her for a moment so she could collect herself. As soon as they were gone, a wisp of green smoke appeared and lured Aurora up a tower to a hidden room.

Slowly, the smoke took the form of a spindle and Maleficent's voice filled the air. "Touch the spindle!" she ordered. Aurora pricked her finger on the spinning wheel and fell into a deep sleep. The only thing that could save her was True Love's Kiss.

Unfortunately, Maleficent had locked the prince in her dungeon. The good fairies found him and discovered that he was Prince Phillip, the same prince who was betrothed to Aurora! They gave him enchanted weapons with which to fight Maleficent. Though the evil fairy changed herself into a fierce dragon, she was no match for the prince's bravery – or the magic sword and shield. He soon defeated her.

Prince Phillip raced to the palace and knelt beside the sleeping beauty. Ever so gently, he kissed her on the lips. He sighed with relief as she opened her eyes and smiled at him.

Soon, a grand, joyous wedding was announced. True love had conquered all!

POCAHONTAS

LISTEN TO YOUR HEART

One day, an adventurous young woman named Pocahontas journeyed deep into the forest to visit Grandmother Willow, an ancient spirit.

Pocahontas told the wise tree that she was troubled by a dream she kept having about a spinning arrow. "It spins faster and faster, until suddenly it stops."

"It seems to me this spinning arrow is pointing down your path," Grandmother Willow replied.

"But what is my path?" wondered Pocahontas. "How am I ever going to find it?"

Grandmother Willow smiled warmly. "All around you are spirits, child," she said. "They live in the earth, the water, the sky. If you listen, they will guide you."

Later, Pocahontas thought about what Grandmother Willow had said. In the distance, she saw something. It was a ship filled with settlers from England.

The next day, Pocahontas spotted a man exploring the forest. His name was John Smith and, like the other men on the ship, he had sailed to this new land in search of gold.

Pocahontas was curious about this man – she had never seen anyone like him before. So she followed him through the woods. Suddenly, he seemed to disappear behind a waterfall. Pocahontas crept out from her hiding place cautiously. Smith jumped through the falls and came face-to-face with the young woman. The two stared at each other for a while. Smith had never seen anyone so beautiful. He moved closer, but Pocahontas was frightened and ran away.

"Wait! Please!" Smith called as he ran after her. "It's all right. I'm not going to hurt you."

Pocahontas hesitated. Leaves swirled around the pair as Smith moved closer and offered her his hand. "Who are you?" he asked.

"I'm Pocahontas," she replied as she took his outstretched hand. When they touched, neither one wanted to let go. In her heart, Pocahontas knew that there was something special about this strange man.

Together, they laughed at Meeko, Pocahontas's mischievous raccoon friend, who rummaged through Smith's bag looking for food.

135

Pocahontas began to sing as she led John Smith through the forest. She showed him how all the parts of nature – animals, plants, the wind, the people – were alive and connected to each other. They watched the gentleness of a mother bear with her cubs. They listened to the wolves cry and saw eagles fly to the top of a sycamore tree.

John Smith began to realize that his people had much to learn. With Pocahontas as his teacher, he could hear the voices of the mountains and even see colours in the wind. He held her hands and gazed into her brown eyes.

Suddenly, drums echoed throughout the forest. Pocahontas looked alarmed.

"What is it?" asked John Smith.

"The drums . . . they mean trouble," she said. "I shouldn't be here."

"Please don't leave," he urged.

"I'm sorry. I have to go," she said and ran off.

Back at the village, Pocahontas's father, Chief Powhatan, warned her to stay close by. "Now is not the time to be running off," he said. He didn't want Pocahontas to get hurt if fighting broke out between the settlers and the Indians.

"Yes, Father," said Pocahontas.

Later, when Pocahontas and her friend Nakoma were gathering corn, John Smith appeared.

"Please don't say anything," Pocahontas whispered to her friend before leaving with Smith.

Nakoma was too shocked to respond. She kept quiet but felt uncomfortable as she watched the two figures disappear into the evening shadows. She had been warned that the settlers were dangerous and was worried about her friend.

Pocahontas led Smith to Grandmother Willow. "Hello, John Smith," the tree said.

John Smith's mouth dropped open. "Pocahontas, that tree is talking to me," he said.

"Then you should talk back," Pocahontas said, smiling.

Grandmother Willow looked kindly into Smith's blue eyes. "He has a good soul," she told Pocahontas, "and he's handsome, too."

John Smith laughed. "Oh, I like her," he said.

Pocahontas was glad the tree spirit approved. After John Smith had left, Grandmother Willow told her that she might have found her path.

Later, when Pocahontas met up with Nakoma, her friend pleaded with her not to see John Smith anymore.

"If you go out there, you'll be turning your back on your own people," Nakoma warned.

"I'm trying to help my people," said Pocahontas.

"Pocahontas, please," Nakoma begged. "You're my best friend. I don't want you to get hurt."

"I won't. I know what I'm doing," replied Pocahontas as she went back into the woods.

But Nakoma wasn't convinced. Concerned about her friend's safety, she sent an Indian warrior named Kocoum to look for Pocahontas in the woods.

Kocoum soon found Pocahontas and Smith. The warrior attacked Smith. All of a sudden, another settler showed up and killed Kocoum!

Furious, other warriors arrived and took John Smith prisoner. He was sentenced to die the next morning.

That night, Pocahontas visited John Smith. "I'm so sorry," she told him, crying. "It would have been better if we'd never met. None of this would have happened."

"Pocahontas, look at me," he said tenderly. "I'd rather die tomorrow than live a hundred years without knowing you."

Pocahontas left and went to see Grandmother Willow. "I feel so lost," she told the tree spirit.

Meeko's ears perked up. The raccoon brought Pocahontas a compass he had taken from John Smith's bag. The arrow on it began to spin.

"It's the arrow from your dream," the tree spirit observed.

"It was pointing to him," Pocahontas said.

"You know your path, child," said Grandmother Willow. "Now follow it."

Pocahontas ran back to the village. Just as John Smith was about to be killed, she stepped in front of him.

"If you kill him, you'll have to kill me, too," she declared to her father. "This is where the path of hatred has brought us. This is the path I choose. What will yours be?"

Everyone stared in stunned silence. Finally, inspired by Pocahontas, the chief ordered the release of John Smith.

But the fighting was not over quite yet. When one of the settlers shot at Pocahontas's father, Smith threw himself in front of the chief and took the bullet himself. In order to have his wound treated, he had to return to London.

Smith looked at Pocahontas. "Come with me?" he asked.

She turned to her father for guidance.

"You must choose your own path," the chief said.

As Pocahontas watched the settlers and Indians begin to share food, she knew what her path must be.

"I'm needed here," she decided.

"Then I'll stay with you," Smith replied.

Pocahontas shook her head. "No. You have to go back," she told him.

"But I can't leave you," he said sadly.

"You never will," she told him. "No matter what happens, I'll always be with you." Then she kissed him good-bye – forever.

As the ship set sail, Pocahontas stood atop a cliff. She was proud that she had listened to her heart, even if it was the hardest thing she had ever done.

Walt Disney's
Snow White
and the Seven Dwarfs

A Royal Visit

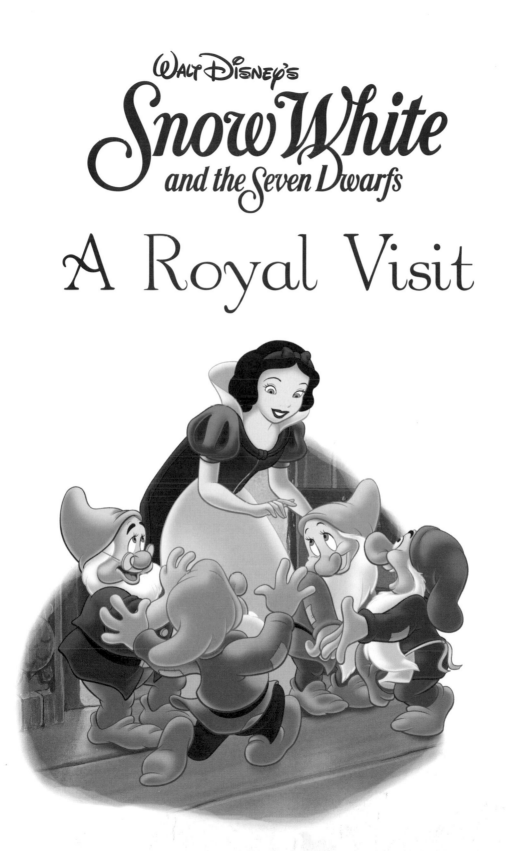

Snow White was just about as happy as a princess could be. She had married her true love, the Prince, and she lived in a beautiful castle. Her wicked stepmother was gone. She had everything she could ever want. But she missed her good friends from the forest, the Seven Dwarfs, very, very much.

"Why do you look so sad, my darling?" the Prince asked Snow White one morning.

"Oh, I've just been thinking about the Dwarfs," she replied. "It's been so long since I've seen them. I really miss them."

"Well, why don't we go for a visit?" the Prince suggested. "Their cottage is not so far away."

"That would be lovely!" Snow White cried. "Let's go today!"

148

While the Prince called the groomsmen to saddle their horses, Snow White wrote a note to tell the Seven Dwarfs that she was coming. Then she asked a bluebird to deliver it.

At the Dwarfs' cottage, Sleepy was just waking up when the bird landed on the windowsill.

"Say, there's a boat in his nose. Er – a note in his toes," said Doc, noticing an envelope in the bird's claws.

"Looks like a . . . a . . . a . . . *ah-choo*," Sneezy said with a sniffle.

"Indeed," Doc replied. "But who could it be from?"

Then, just as he reached for the letter, the scent of sweet perfume drifted to his nose.

"Why, it's from Snow White!" Doc exclaimed. He and Sneezy and Sleepy ran downstairs to tell the others.

Doc began to read the note. "'My dear Dwarfs,'" he said. "Heh-heh, she calls us 'dear'!"

"Oh, get on with it!" grumbled Grumpy.

Doc scanned the note. "Well, um . . . well, golly gee! She's comin' for a visit! Today!" he cried.

"Hooray!" Happy cheered. "Snow White is coming!"

But the other six Dwarfs looked around their messy cottage. Dirty dishes and clothes were piled everywhere.

Doc handed a broom to Dopey. "We have a lot to do, men! Sleepy, you bake – er, *make* the beds. Bashful, you fold the clothes. Sneezy, you dust the furniture. Dopey will sweep the doors – er, *floors*."

"She's comin' at *noon*!" Grumpy huffed. "She'll want lunch. Someone's gonna have to cook!"

"Why don't you and Happy fix somethin' suitable for Snow White to eat?" Doc suggested.

The Dwarfs started to work on their chores right away. It didn't go very well.

Sleepy got tired and lay down in the middle of Grumpy's bed. Sneezy kept sneezing as he dusted. And Dopey knocked furniture over as he swept.

Meanwhile, Happy and Grumpy couldn't agree on what kind of sandwiches to make.

"Snow White likes peanut butter and jelly, I know," Happy declared.

"She likes ham and cheese," Grumpy grumbled. "Everyone knows that."

By the time Doc finally got them to agree on something, the clock struck twelve and there was a soft rap on the door.

"They're . . . ahh . . . ahh . . . *heeere*!" Sneezy sneezed. "Wake up, Sleepy!"

The Dwarfs ran to the door and opened it. Their beloved princess was here! They smiled as Snow White hugged each of them and kissed their foreheads. "How I've missed you all!" she cried.

"Please forgive the mess, Princess," Bashful whispered to her. "We didn't quite get it cleaned up."

"Oh, please," Snow White said with a laugh, "forgive *me* for giving you such short notice! Besides, I've come to see *you* – not your cottage."

"Would you care for a ham-and-jelly sandwich?" Doc offered, holding up a platter. "Or peanut butter and cheese?"

"Oh, how sweet," Snow White kindly replied. "But . . . well . . . you see . . ." She paused. "If I had known you'd go to all this trouble, I wouldn't have brought a picnic with me."

"Picnic?!" the Dwarfs exclaimed.

"Well, yes. I remembered how much you liked it when I cooked, so I brought some of your favourites."

Just then, the Prince walked in with an overflowing basket.

"What did you bring?" Doc asked hopefully.

"Oh, just some roast chicken and deviled eggs," Snow White said. "Cinnamon bread and butter. Corn and tomatoes from the

royal garden. Sugar cookies, cinnamon cookies and a fresh apple pie. . . . But let's eat your sandwiches first."

The Dwarfs looked at one another and Doc cleared his throat. "We can have ham and jelly any time," he said. "Let's enjoy your picnic and have a great visit."

And that's exactly what they did.